S-7 CHRONICLES
OPERATION SOLAR FLARE:
A TOP SECRET MISSION

LEWIS COLIN

Ordering Information:

Prime Seven Media
518 Landmann St.
Tomah City, WI 54660

Printed in the United States of America

SHAMURIA'S SEVEN SECRET SERVICE SYNTHETIC SOLAR SOLDIERS

S7

7 = COMPLETE

8 = NEW BEGINNINGS

OPERATION SOLAR FLARE: A TOP SECRET MISSION

CHARACTERS

1. Shaila – Captain & Operations Leader
2. Ciara – Logistics/ Computer Analyst
3. Justice – legal Analyst - Twin
4. Justin – Technical & Mechanical - Twin
5. Randy – Transportation & Mechanical
6. Brock – Tactical & Weapons Support
7. Briana – Doctor/Medical, Psychological and Solar Scientist.

CONCEPT

Shamuria put together a secret team of operatives to find out who is responsible for destroying all life in three other solar systems.

After Shamuria is destroyed the team searches for a new home which turn out to be earth.. The team desperately fights to protect earth and the Milky Way from a similar fate.

Their synthetic humanoid bodies are transformed due to living on alien planet earth.. They inherently merge abilities, education, talent, skiH and develop seven powers each.

1. Telepathy
2. Teleportation
3. Telekinesis
4. Invisibility
5. Invincibility
6. Flight
7. Super Strength

Plus one individual power that distinguishes them one from the other.

1. Speed
2. Fire
3. Laser
4. Ice
5. Electric
6. Morph
7. Galactic Languages

CHAPTER 1

FURY'S FIRE

octor Collier, I have the final analysis on the S7 trials ready for review. Thank you Margret, please place those analyses on my desk. I will begin the seventh and final phase of the project in three linear marks. Right doctor consider it done. Thank you. Have Triell set the alabaster and juniper boxes as well. Will do sir. Ah, Doctor Collier, we see you fail to terminate your research as ordered. This sort of insubordination will definitely not help your cause. My cause senator is to save the whole of Shamuria, don't you understand that? Without S7 Shamuria will perish. No other scientific data support your findings Doctor. Marcilla, Ardren and all the other solar kilts were eons and eons away. There is nothing to suggest that we are in imminent danger or any other sort of threat to Shamuria, neither its moons nor the tri-sun star. We are absolutely safe and secure here. Besides Decca Global and it's scientific team has created the Latmos Kilt's Sphere which protects all of Shamuria and the outer quadrants as far as Phoenix Yuthka. Senator please listen to me, I have the final analysis ready for review. Doctor no one, I mean no one cares about your final analysis. A decision has been reached already. We have gone forward with operation rekindle. But Senator, pleading his case. No doctor, I will no longer tolerate the babblings of a foolish has been. Nona set cosmos to course 8547211 please. I need to take a retreat. Yes senator as you wish. Margret, somehow I have to make them understand that their analysis are wrong. I will support you in any way I can Doctor. Activate S7. Doctor, we haven't finished the final phase as you've suggested doctor. What if S7 fails? We will not have another opportunity like this again. If we don't, Shamuria will not survive until fifty linear marks more. In fact that's just a guess Margret. I really can't pin point the exact time of Fury's Fire.

Alert! Alert! Security Alert! Alert! Alert! Security Alert! This is not a drill.

Alert! Alert! Security Alert! Alert! Alert! Security Alert! This is not a drill.

Alert! Alert! Security Alert! Alert! Alert! Security Alert! This is not a drill.

What is it Doctor? Margret I fear we are too late. Have you activated S7? Yes Doctor, It has already been done for three atron cycles. Good Margret, now deploy the deflector shields until we can get S7 into orbit. But doctor you are a life being, you must accompany the vessel. No, all none life beings will shut down soon and only a life being will be able to insure they reach orbit intact. Fury's Fire has begun. Doctor Collier, what is this Security Alert. I'm sorry senator; the end has come for Shamuria. That is impossible! It can't be. AH the scientific data stated otherwise. Why didn't you say something nor do something. There is nothing left to do senator. Hopefully someone will learn of this incident and they will be able to save themselves from a similar fate. God speed S7. God speed. Meanwhile, aboard the S7 galactic vessel Nena, Doctor comer's synthetic intelligence squad is being awakened just point five light shards away from fury's fire. Shaila, this is Nena, awaken protocol number one. Captain Shaila Collier operations leader reporting for duty Nena. Captain your memory data processor has been informed. Yes, Nena. I have all data filed. Now awaken Shamuria's Seven Secret Service Synthetic Solar Soldiers. Ciara Collier, logistics and computer analyst reporting for duty Nena. Brock Collier, tactical & weapons support at your service Nena. Doctor Breana Collier, Medical, psychiatric and solar scientist reporting for duty Nena. Randy Collier, Transportation and Mechanical reporting for duty Nena. Justin Collier, Technical and mechanical reporting for duty Nena. Justice Collier, Legal Analyst reporting for duty Nena. All S7 authority is relinquished from Nena to Shaila by order of Doctor Almar Collier. Thank you Nena, now begin S7 Chronicles. As you wish Shaila. S7, I am Doctor Almar Collier a solar scientist of the Shamuria research institute west lunar tri-sun. About 30 earth years ago,

Ardren our sister galaxy was destroyed by what we can only assume was a solar flare of Dartarius their blue sun. At least fifty years prior to that incident their scientist along with ours of Shamuria was searching for an alternate Kilt in which life could be supported. We have found one such place two million galaxies away. There is no way for life to sustain itself at the speeds necessary to reach this kilt. Our only hope would be to create a synthetic life form to carry hope across the multiverse to warn others who are in the path of destruction. Once the fury fire began it has become a domino effect. Margret my assistant and I studied the kilt earth so that you will blend with their life beings seamlessly. So, I am now speaking to you in English one of their principle languages. You will find that they are much like life beings on our Kilt. Let us do all that we can to prevent a premature destruction of their galaxy the Milky Way. You have at least ten earth years to stop fury's fire annihilation. Each of you have been equipped with several abilities that will enable you to perform at your maximum levels for one thousand earth years. There is a uni- sun which is a great energy source there. Margret and I were unable to conclude exactly how you will interact with this sun opposed to our own tri-sun. Again we know you are compatible but not sure if it will have any adverse effects. Shaila! Yes Nena. There is large debris from the explosion off the aft stern. On it Shaila, Nena power up ships weapons now. On-line Brock, said Nena. Randy, I'm ready for tactical maneuvers. Right Brock got it covered. We are approaching the Beiing Nebular. Thanks Ciara, said Nena. Captain, permission to begin evasive maneuvers? Permission granted Randy. Just get us out of here. Ciara! Yes Captain? Do a re-route and then put us back on course. Already done captain. Brock! Go Nena. Destruction of approaching debris to starboard rear has failed. I will defend. Fading through the ship's exterior, Brock uses his electric pulse. Then he races toward the massive rock with light speed and super human strength and collides with the object shattering it into a trillion pieces saving Nena and S7. Did you see that? How did he do that? I don't know Justice. Brock, how did you know you could do that? I don't know Justin, it just happened. Ciara. Yes Nena. That blast carried us five light shards away from the Andromeda galaxy. We are nearing our destination. Yes Ciara, I know. Then we must prepare for earth now Shaila. Affirmative Ciara. Doctor Collier your presence is requested on the bridge. I am here Nena. Yes Shaila you have summoned me. Breana what do you know of the life beings of earth? I will telepathically download each of you for your briefing. Then we must master a humanoid identity. It is necessary to change our metal alloy covering to Nano molecular isotopes which will resemble the humanoid skin. The metal alloy will act as a skeletal frame inside. So in essence we will be inside out. Not quite, but something like that. When will this transformation be applicable Breana? Soon Shaila, I am working out the final details right now. I have to come up with a solution for what the humans call hair. Not quite sure how to replicate it yet. Hair? What is this hair? Well, the females of the species are adorned by it and their male counterparts can as well. However, most males usually wear it close to their vodes or heads as the humans say. It comes in lots of colors too. Usually black, brown, red or Blonde. I wm choose Black. What color will you choose Shaila? I think I wm choose red. Excellent choice, Shaila. And You Justice? I'm not sure. Let Ciara chose next. What! Why! Please make a choice girls, said Shaila. Okay, I will have blonde. That leaves brown for you Justice. I don't care, just as long as I don't have to make a choice. What if I chose the wrong color and it looks hideous. You silly girl, I will insure that we are all beautiful earth girls. Justin, since you and Justice are twin beings, you will have the same hair color. Brock and Randy, want to make a choice? I don't care just as Bong as I don't look heinous. Okay, I will surprise you. At any rate, the earth beings often change hair colors. So, if any of you decide to change you can. It will beset as part of our programming as well. Let's get down to the good part now ladies and gents. Tactical and weapon ology. We will all train for two hours beginning at 0300 hrs. Each day from now until we reach Earth Kilt. Ciara will be responsible for all academic exercises, with the exception of psych and science. The good doctor will handle that area. Thank you Brock. I just want to say this mission was very important to Doctor Collier and his team. We will not let them down. As being the eldest among you, it is my responsibility to insure your safety. You will comply with all S7 protocol as has been mandated by Doctor Collier. Any infractions will be met with the strictest of punishments allowable. Being that we are siblings will not cause me to hesitate in performing my duties as your captain. In order to prevail in our mission to serve and protect earth kilt we must govern ourselves with the utmost respect for life. We will work secretively among them as this is for their own protection. No one outside of Nena, must know our real identities if at all possible. Our abilities must not be shown openly or in our alternate states. This is for the protection of those whom we will work with on a day to day basis. Are you orders dear? All saying, unanimously yes. Now let the modulation take place. S7, metamorphoses begin. With the blare of colorful lights filling Nena from bow to stern, S7 take on a more human form. Wow, Ciara, you look awesome. So do you Justice. We all do. Are we now as fragile as the life beings of earth kilt? No, we only look similar outwardly. Nothing can penetrate our exoteric camouflage. It is very important that we regenerate as to be fully prepared for the mission ahead. Right Shaila, we will dock earth eighteen hours according to their time. Maintain your current course Nena. Will do Captain comer. Alright everyone to your quarters. AH hands are expected to be on deck in fourteen hours. Yes captain. By the way Breana, great job. Thank You Captain. During a ten hour reanimation period for S7, Nena goes through a morph of her own brought on by the sun. She is now able to become any mode of transportation or dwelling S7 will need. She can duplicate any of their individual powers as well as their cumulative powers. However, she is still only their adjutant. She is the supreme adjutant. She can now foster a host of other lesser mechanical parts to provide support to the team as needed. These parts can also take on human form, but only for short periods of time. These parts can be destroyed and also replaced by elements of metalliferous earth and a few kilts of Andromeda. The sound of a ship's whistle wakes the crew of Nena to a brand new life on earth kilt. Finally we are here. Yes, earth kilt is very beautiful. Planet earth ladies. This is what they call it. We must use only earth's languages from here on out. Got it? Got It. You will refer to me as Shaila. Captain is understood. We will only revert during covert operations. The year is 2741. The city we are in is New Persepolis. Persepolis is a metropolis. People have migrated from all around to be here. It is believed to be the largest city ever built. Shaila a lot has changed here on earth since our last analyses from Shamuria. Yes, Ciara this was caused by a drastic move of the earth's crust. This will take place every so many eons. I guess that explains the one large mass of land and a few islands here and there. It is still quite lovely though isn't it? Yes, yes it is. Alright soldiers, let's get to it now. We have our work cut out for us. Justin! Look! What is that? It is some kind of a probe Justice, stand still. I think it is trying to read my aura. Don't moved twins, because I can read its aura. It can't make out exactly what you are. Stand perfectly still via telepathy. We don't want to antagonize it. Okay Breana we understand. I will fly away to see if it will follow and then Justin you must destroy it. I don't know about this Breana, maybe we should contact the others. No time Justice, just trust me sister. Okay. Gone in the twinkle of an eye, the probe was not even aware for at least a moment that she was not there. In panic the probe turns to search for Breana, while Breana speaks via telepathy to the twins instructing them to cloak their exoteric with invisibility. The images are being transmitted back to a military headquarters in central Persepolis. Great job twins, now let's report back to Nena. Shaila and the others have to be warned. Meanwhile back at the camp. Randy what are you doing? I'm testing my electric orbs. Check this out Shaila. Showing off his electric capabilities. You think that's something, watch and learn. Moving at the speed of light. That's the spazz girl. Shaila, Brock, we've got trouble. Already? It's not what you think. We came across a probe. A probe? What do you mean a probe? It was trying to read my aura Randy. Ciara was too hot and hard to handle. We got rid of it, but I don't think we have seen the last of it. Troops we need to make our way to Persepolis now. Gather only what you need and let's go. How far is it to the city? It will take us awhile traveling the way earth life beings travel. Maybe a day or so. What. We are really going to do this? Yes, of course. Remember your oath. Yeah right, the oath. Come on let's be sharp. We have to really get down to business. Where do you think the probe came from? That's a very good question. Maybe we should go back and see if we can trace it to its origins. That's a good idea. Only this time we will be ready. Brock and Breana your up. Ciara take them to the spot and make sure to cloak yourselves. Let's go girls. Twins go to work. Justice I need every bit of information regarding the judicial system in Persepolis, synthesize everyone so that we will be on one accord. Also share with Nena. Roger

Captain. Justin stream ahead about a mile or so under cloak and shield. Keep your eyes peeled. Roger that captain. Randy bring the virtual view reels up and synthesize the feed to everyone please, thank you. Alright Shaila running virtual view. Nena smooth out this ride a little will you. I want to be fit for a fight if one ensues. Captain Persepolis dead ahead north by north west. Good. There seems to be some type of festivities going on right now. Oh yes, the festival of Awa Odori. It is of Japanese descent. We have reached the town of New Shibuya. Anyone up for a good time? We are not here for a good time. Blend in with the surroundings and learn what you can of their culture. Don't be such an ole lady captain. Don't you know how to shake a tail feather? Seriously Randy, you have got to tone it down a bit. Oh alright, but no one heard. Besides, if we are too careful, people wm be suspicious. I suppose you are right on that account. Just remember to meet back here in one hour. That's Affirmative Shaila. That's definitely affirmative. Curiosity will kill the cat at that. I better find a place to communicate with the others. Shaila we are all here. You forget your telepathy. Yes, I suppose I have at that. How are things there? Fine, we have located the probe and are in route to its origins. I will keep you posted. Randy do control yourself. Cram it sister. Not everyone has the telepathy thing down yet. Temper, temper brother. I just want to have a little fun is all?

CHAPTER 2

The probe has landed Ciara. Brock, let's take a closer look. We should teleport inside while still under cloak to examine the origins. On my mark and five, four,three,two,one. Inside the underground bunker. A full military base is hidden just five miles south of Persepolis. Shaila, we have infiltrated an underground city. There appear to be soldiers of some sort. Everything you can think of is here. Why is this necessary? Are they afraid of something or someone? Its hard to say. Let's seek out leaders. I will take the East quadrant and Brock you take the west. Bre. Sure, I'll take the north. Meet back here in thirty minutes. Communicating via telepathy. Brock, do you have anything yet? No. How about you? Nothing. Bre, how are you doing? I think I hit the jack pot. What do you mean? I mean, the leaders are in the north quadrant in a top secret meeting. Apparently a transmission reached the earth about 740 years ago from Ardren. Maybe about 10 years before it was destroyed. On earth it would have been around 2001. That is exactly right Brock. We will teleport to you. Tune in to my life vibe, it will bring you directly to me. Well, what else did you here? That's about it so far. I got here while the meeting was already in progress. Gentlemen we all know that earth will eventually expire. We simply can't support all life out in space. We will have to decide who will live and who will die. No man should have the ability to pass that kind of judgment on mankind. I agree with you, Chancellor. That's why we are all here. We have to decide together. That is absolutely barbaric. All of you troglodytes would dare take another man's life to save his own. Look at it this way chancellor, some life will survive. There are literally billions of lives we are talking about. And millions can be saved. Chancellor, we want some of our children and grandchildren to carry on human life. If we could save everyone man, woman, and child we would. The constellation of Libra is about twenty light years away and Gliese 581 is our only hope. We just don't have enough raw material left to furnish a trip for billions that alone multiple trips. It's just not possible. Chancellor please understand what our cause is. How will we decide? One thing we can do is send the most premier minds the earth can gather and ship them off. This will give them a fighting chance for survival once they have encountered life on new earth. We still have another twenty years to gather our collective analyses of data so to begin our quest for new earth. Guys are you hearing this? Yes Randy. Shaila, are you in tune with us? Shaila. Are you there? This cavern must be too deep for us to communicate with the others. Nena can you hear us. Yes Breana, I can hear you and will relay this intel to Shaila at once. Thank you Nena. Always a pleasure Ciara. Brock, Breana, Ciara simultaneous call from Nena. Shaila would like for everyone to meet here asap. Ten-four. Let's go ladies. After you Bro. Two hours later at S7 headquarters. They intercepted a communication ripple from Ardren back in 2001. They are aware of the threat to them. They are planning to leave earth in about twenty years. At least, they have a plan of escape in case we fail. But that's just it, they don't know about us. Yeah, and we need to keep it that way. Of course this gives us the advantage. How so Shaila? We have to make sure that our technical advances are matched with what they have as to give them an edge. There is really no way to stop a solar flare. Perhaps we won't have to stop it. Maybe we can just divert it. These people are using all of their resources to vacate this planet. Look at her, she is so alive. Yes and so was Shamuria and now there is nothing left. Perhaps we can send Nena back to gather Intel for us from Shamuria that will help us with the earth's dilemma. Perhaps, but not anytime soon. There is still much to learn about the earth. We have only been here a day and we have gathered some great Intel. Nena, I will need you to run some hypothesis on how our makeup is faring in this atmosphere opposed to our host. Already began analysis upon arrival. Good job Nena. Always a pleasure to serve. Download all findings to us severally Nena. Will do captain. Knowing these people have time gives us time as well. I think we may need some of the life beings to assist us in our efforts Shaila. Eventually we will have to learn to trust others. Yes, I agree. We have to take our time though. Timing is everything Breana. Timing is everything. This is only the beginning of our quest to assist earth. Tomorrow we will go among them again and forge an alliance serially until we have earned their trust. Once we have established trust amongst our new peers then we can work tirelessly until fury1s fire burns no more. I took notice to their attire. I think we kind of stood out a bit. Yes, I do believe you are right dear sister. It seems we are a little dated in our attire. I suppose we will need to do a bit of shopping in New Shibuya. Wonderful. How exquisite Shaila? My thoughts exactly. Believe me dear girl I know. How will we get into the secret chambers to meet the elite among them Shaila? Are we to be common people or counted as the elite? We will be working class people with varying careers that will allow us entry into the lifestyles of the most elite. That's why you're the oldest. You're so smart. It is my individual makeup Justice. Okay, everyone needs to pipe down for the evening. We have an early start tomorrow with tactical and weapon ology. Do we have to Brock? We can just do a synthetic download and be done with it. Yes, that's true. But we want to appear as human as possible, so we must do as the humans do. Great Shamuria's pieces, he is a genius now. He is right twins; we have to blend in better. Another thing Breana, I think we are just a little too flawless. There were no life beings like us. They all had some problem or another. That's completely unavoidable Shaila. We are not able to duplicate these abnormalities in their human makeup. The new attire will do wonders for a tone down. Trust me. Hum, yes trust is the operative word isn1 t it. Now, did anyone have a change of heart about hair color or anything like that? No, I think we all look fine. I agree. So if all agree say yeah. Yeahhhh.

Good then that's settled. The life beings sleep. I saw an offspring resting and the mother and another female said they sleep all the time. Since we are practicing to be like them will we sleep? Shaila. Yes Nena. With your permission, I would like to speak. Certainly, go ahead. As part of my analysis of your adaptation to earth, you are all becoming more human like as time goes on. You will require sleep as the sun goes down and rises. This is how your life span here can double or even triple. Doctor Collier thought it would be approximately one thousand years of life in your core cell. But my new findings show differently because we are actually here. I can pin point it accurately. Again if you apply the sleep process as the humans, your life span will increase. Thank you Nena. What will be the use of all that time? We can still help others even after fury's fire has passed earth. I don't know if that's all I want to do in existence. You are beginning to develop a conscience. Doctor Collier would be proud. Although you will never truly be a life being you will become its closes relative. Because of the special alloy that is contained in you, you will always remain synthetic inwardly. Humans have referred to us as cyborgs. I believe the idea of cyborgenics is more acceptable to mankind today than it was many years ago. None the less we are different from them. The issue may even be that we are alien rather than cyborgenic now anyway. Team let's not draw conclusions here of what the perception of the life beings will be until we reach that point. We are just investigating them to learn more about their way of life today opposed to our assumptions about who we think they are. This is why it is crucial that we remain anonymous until we are sure. Shaila, we have to be more aggressive in our pursuit of galactic welfare for the people of the multiverse. Ciara, we all have accepted the same pledge and are pursuant of it diligently. Regardless of the world's view point of us, we will eventually have to act. Exactly. So why are we then hesitant to approach them with these real issues? It is their lives that we are ordered to save. We must believe in the cause in which our father created us. Shaila we need to stand unified knowing that we are doing the right thing. When you do that very thing that you are created to do, that makes whatever we will endure worthwhile. I'm ready to act upon the ordinances which are written upon my heart. I am my father's daughter. I am Ciara Collier. And you, you sister. You are Shaila Collier. Leader of our kind. We will not fail. All we need to do is believe in ourselves. Come on you and you (Justin & Justice). Randy, Breana and Brock. We are more than capable of finishing this course if we faint not. Do you believe it? Than act on it. With our hearts of fire kindled against our foe, we shall prevail against it. All the while chanting the cause of her heart, she is floating away unaware of her state. The others are watching in amazement and agreement as she glides high across the plains and valleys above New Shibuya. Then suddenly a whish across the sky. What was that? I don't know. Let's get it. Over there. No over here. Split up, it's more than one. Right. Lets ready our force fields. Justin. Yes Justice, I'll go to the left here. Alright. Be careful Justice. Likewise. Whispering via telepathy. Ciara are you over here? Randy, anybody here? Attacked from behind, Ciara has no chance to fight off a surprise capture. Also being underground adds no hope of calling for backup. Thinking to herself, no one knows I'm here. Nena can you hear me? Unable to pick up a response, Ciara is filled with anxiety. Placed in a hole deep under the earth in a four feet by 3 feet steel entrapment with her eyes covered, feet and hands bound. This is a first for her and she has never been alone in a tough situation like this. Also her strength becomes dull because of a lack of exposure to the sun. Back on the surface the others are still tracking the probes and looking for answers regarding their origins, unaware there is a problem ensuing. Justin and Justice captured one probe and Breana and Brock has tracked another to its origins, the same military facility they have encountered before. Hours have gone by and still no one is aware that Ciara has gone missing. Justin and Justice return to Nena to regroup with the others for a conference, then and only then did they realize that Ciara was not accounted for. Where is Ciara? I don't know, we thought she was with one of you. No, we all thought she was with the two of you. Well where can she be? Immediately the team forms two search parties to trace their sisters' whereabouts. Shaila, Justice and Justin make up the first search party, while Randy, Breana and Brock make up the second. Team A return to the last place anyone recall seeing Ciara, where the probes appeared to them. While team B, returned to the military facility. Meanwhile Nena has returned to orbit to be closer to the sun to harvest its energy to leverage the team's capabilities. I feel my strength increasing. Yes, you're right, so do I. Chime in to the others as we are able to communicate via telepathy for greater distances now. Brock, Bre, I am getting a faint signal over here. The vibe has to be Ciara. Yes, the closer I get, I since the same. Why is the signal so weak? I don't know, but I believe we have to act fast. Right. Nena copies that and so does the others. Randy, we are on our way to provide backup. Do what you must to save our sister. Ten-Four Captain. Team ready force fields. Ready. Invisibility and go. Via telepathy. Brock, you and I will provide cover while Bre handles the rescue over. Copy over. I'm downloading my morph abilities to you Bre. And my electric as well sis. Thanks boys. It will come in handy. Passing through the earth at light speed the team reaches Ciara's tomb. Hold on Ciara we are here. With a blast of electrical energy, the tomb gives way and Breana morphs into a giant phoenix, while employing the power of fire, speed, flight, invisibility, super human strength ,and laser to free herself and Ciara from the depths of the earth racing toward Nena and the sun. While Brock and Randy wage an all-out war with the probes. The two combine to become one fighting force. Their combined abilities include all seven commonalities, telepathy, teleportation, Flight, telekinesis, invisibility, invincibility, and super human strength times two. And Randy's electrical powers as well as Brock's ability to morph into any object inanimate or living. This is a first for the siblings. Brock and Randy become Brandy. A fierce battle droid. No longer in human form, with the silver metal alloy visible.

Detecting no life beings in the sector, Brandy annihilates the entirety of sector one while in tactical mode within seconds. The military sentries were no match for the alien droid. Because Brandy has never been exposed to the sun, no transformation has taken place and he appears in his archaic form. Seperating prior to reaching the surface, Brandy remains unaffected by the sun. Brock and Randy fully aware of the devastation Brandy has caused. I am not sure what to think of that. Me either. He was both awesome and scary all at the same time. Yes. We have to be careful the next time we implore him. Yes brother. I did not have full control of my faculties there. Neither did I. Let's meet with the other aboard Nena to discuss what just happened here. You are right. Teleport now. Breana, where is Ciara? How is she doing? She is still very weak. Nena has her cocooned in the holistphere. Nena, any new developments? No, she is still quite fragile. We are here. Hi, Shaila. Where is Ciara? She is currently in the holistsphere. Nena, can you repair the damage. Yes, she will need much rest and direct interaction with the uni-sun to fully recuperate. Brock and Randy meet me in my quarters now. I felt an unusual voluminous energy before. Either of you want to explain that? Yes. It was Brandy. Who or what is Brandy? We are not sure. He is both Brock and I combined. I'm not sure exactly how it happened, but we joined and became an altogether separate individual. I'm listening. Tell me everything that happened. Nena. I'm recording the S7 chronicles always. Thank you. Proceed, Randy. Well, we became over whelmed and were outnumbered. The probes were firing there lasers and other arsenal of weapons upon us and suddenly with synchronized thought we implored him. Shaila, he just was. We didn't intend for it to happen nor do we understand how it happened. It just did. Okay, Brock, I understand. You are not in any real trouble. I will restrict you to Nena, until we can determine exactly what this is. Nena, your analyses. While it was not a foreign cause. It was very violent. As much as I can determine, this is something Dr. Collier intended for S7 to do. I simple believe that this Brondy has not been exposed to the sun. Therefore, he had no knowledge of the collective and its cause. So, then Brandy is ignorant. Yes. He acted out of survival mechanisms which we all have. He simply was protecting himself from the probes. I believe that Brandy is only one of many different synthetic beings existing. There can be any number of combinations of possible synthetic beings emerge at any time. So in essence, the result would be different if I were to combine with Brock or Randy. Yes. Each individual can combine with any other individual and a personality will emerge. I see. Also you can each combine and there would be another. You mean all three of us. Yes, any combinations all the way up to seven or possible eight. Eight? Yes, including myself. I believe it is imperative that we leave the Milky Way and run test trials in the Andromeda quadrants to keep the life beings of earth safe. Yes, I agree. There is no time like the present. Alert all members and begin the teleportation process immediately. What about Ciara? As long as she is aboard she will naturally comply. There is no need to wake her as all will be downloading to her by the collective. Alright then, that settles it. Synchronizing all energy the crew moves Nena across the galaxy to the Andromeda quadrant via teleportations. Still able to draw energy required from Andromeda, the team units to become a single synthetic Droid. Cartel Nena Collier is formed. 57 - CNC. I am 57 - CNC. I know and understand the mission of 57 and the collective as it has been down loaded to me. I am the completed version of the fighting soldier for the multiverse created by Dr. Collier who serves the Omnipotent One, creator of all that is. Cartel Nena has all the abilities of the collective and Nena times eight. She appears as an alloy droid and in synthetic human form. She can be as large as fifty feet tall and as small as a human toddler. She is the team's ultimate secret weapon. The collective is very pleased. She teleports back to the outer reaches of the Milky Way to draw upon the energy of the sun. The results are no changes as she is fit for duty. She teleports back out to the Andromeda Quadrant for phase two of the test trials, first morphing back to the collective, then taking Nena out of the equation, the seven combine to form Solera. I am Solera the collective of the seven. I am ready for duty Nena. Then teleport to the outer reaches of the Milky Way and await my orders. The next phase reveals a triune of Randy, Brock and Justin called Tristan. Then Tristan combined with Nena became Bran. In the next phase, the four girls combine to become Anu. Anu and Nena combine to become Destiny. Tristan and Anu are twins and so are Destiny and Bran. Bran and Destiny combine is also S7 - CNC. Tristan and Anu combined is Solera. Of course Brandy is Brock and Randy. However, Brock and Justin become Dano. Justin and Randy become Lito. Quato is a combination of Brondy and Nena. Dano and Nena become Daneno. And Lito and Nena become Litone. Brock alone combined with Nena became Belnah. Randy and Nena became Rah. Justin and Nena combine are Jah. The combinations are endless, for example, Shaila and Breana together are Sildah. Juno is a combination of Justice and Shaila. Justice and Ciara became Ceta, while Breana and Ciara are Tera. Ciara and Shaila are Milcah, while Justice and Breana are Breta. Breana and Nena are Zera. While Ciara and Nena are Cena. Justice and Nena become Ellana, while Shaina is a combination of Shaila and Nena. Now Shaila and Brock are Dru. Shaila and Randy are Dax. Then there is JuNe a combo of Shaila and Justin. Nu is Justin and Justice, while Ju is Breana and Brock. Theres Royce, which is Justice and Brock, while Justice and Randy became Taylor. Breana and Justin are Rum, while Breana and Randy are Brandy. Ciara and Randy is Rae, but Ciara and Justin is Tee. And then there's the combination of Ciara and Brock which is Lah. Again these combinations go on and on. End of test and trials took several days. S7 has learned a lot about their several abilities. This will enable them to move on to the next level of integration with the life beings on earth.

'm having a hard time understanding why the life beings attacked Ciara? I don't think it was a random thing. Justice we have the take into consideration, they do not realize we are here. In fact, I believe they are only defending themselves against an invasion. We are their allies. Yes, we are, but they don't have a clue that we are. You're right Breana. We have to gain friends in order to blend in. We will all go back to New Persepolis. What good will that do Shaila? I don't have all the answers, but we have to start somewhere, and New Persepolis is where all the action has been. We will introduce ourselves as the Collier kids from some other region. Somewhere like Perdida. Exactly, Perdida is over the North Mountains and people rarely cross from one area to the other. That is perfect. let's see, we can claim the township of Hatra. No, no, how about New Memphis. Right, that's it, New Memphis. That will explain our good health and extremely good looks. Sure and our parent are deceased killed in world war three. Brock, that all sounds very good. Synchronize that information, now down load. I will establish myself as an ex-militant, Captain Shaila Collier. I will be known as Dr. Breana Collier, with no emphasis on a particular degree. Yes, that's good. If we only refer to you as a doctor, no one will think to ask a doctor of what. Maybe or maybe not, but it's all good. Justin and Justice can act as the younger siblings. Grad students if you will. Justin a mechanical engineer and Justice a student of the law. Randy, like me was in the military in aviation. Ciara will be the civil engineer, while Brock will represent all law enforcement. We can use these skills to interact with those assigned these duties and forge allies. It won't be that simple. We all have our work cut out for us, but we must always be with a partner so that what happened to Ciara will never happen again. We can say that we need work in these fields and see if there are available positions in these areas. Shaila, there are availabilities in each of the necessary fields. I will plug each of you in as applicants now. Your resumes have been downloaded. I have also taken the liberty of creating the necessary documentation required by law. Good, Good. All that is left is to do it. Well it is about three o'clock earth time, so we need to regenerate for tomorrow. I will complete all down loads to each of you individually while you regenerate. Thank You, Nena. You are welcomed. Always a pleasure to serve. S7, arise the new day is dawning. We are in the earth's orbit and I will assume the role of your dwelling. The entire crew is feeling a little jittery about the assignment, so Shaila asked Breana to come up with something to calm them down. All hands gather to the port side of Nena for roll call. Justice. Present. Justin. Here . Brock. Here. Ciara. Here. Randy. Present. Shaila. Here. Okay everyone, today is the first day of the rest of your lives. This is where you pull up your britches and show um whose boss. There is simply nothing to fear, but fear itself. And we all know the opposite of fear is love. We are here because of love. What do we want to do? We want to share that love we have with the life beings. Sooo, are you ready? Yes you are ready. Ready for what? Ready to love and be loved. Now shake it off and breathe in slowly. And exhale. And again. And let it out slowly. Now we are out of here. Hi my name is Brock. I am here for an appointment with Sgt. Kellogg. Oh yes, please take a seat. Sitting in the lobby with ten other candidates. Mrs. Burns, I am Justin and this is my sister Justice. We are transfer students from the University of New Memphis. Welcome to the University of New Shibuya. We hope that our campus will meet all of your academic needs. Good morning, my name is Shaila Collier and I need assistance finding employment. I have just move here from New Memphis, Perdida. Randy Collier. Yes, I'm here. Mr. Collier, please follow me? Dan Worthington will see you now. Doctor Collier, it is a pleasure to meet you. The feeling is mutual sir. I am looking forward to speaking with you regarding your research on quantum physics. We here at Murray's Research Institute are excited about your thesis. Collier. Ciara Collier. Yes, that's me. Jonathan Brooks will see you now. Ms. Collier, come on in and seat down. I received your application for employment with Dexter, Lance & Holt. We pride ourselves as being the top Computer Scientist in all of Persepolis. Yes, I know. That is why I sought you out. My family and I have recently moved here from New Memphis and are making a fresh start. A fresh start, you say. Yes. Some years ago, our parents were killed in world war three. My eldest sister Shaila and the second oldest Randy both joined the military to support us while the rest of us finished school. It will be a great pleasure to work with such an elite group of scientist. I won't let you down. Very well then young lady, you have a job. Really. Yes. When can you start? Right away. How about tomorrow morning then. That will be just great. Thank you, very much Mr. Brooks. You want regret it. Indeed Ciara, the pleasure is truly all mines. Ciara. Ciara. Hello Breana. Hi. How did your interview go? It went very well. In fact, I am to report to work tomorrow morning. So am I. Let's go home and see how the others fared. Sure thing. Wait, I want to look thru some of the magazines to check out the latest fashion trends. Don't worry; I have it all set up at home with Nena. Cool beans. Besides, I have some really snazzy things lined up for me and I want your opinion. Sure. Girls. Hello everyone. We have great news. So, I suppose we all have great news. If you mean did we all find work, the answer is yes. I will be going to the police academy for training in a week. Justice and I have been accepted into the University as well. I have a license as a private investigator thru Welch Investigative Services. Well that will help explain the snooping around. Yes exactly. With the exception of Brock, everyone will begin their new jobs tomorrow. I have arranged for us to do a night on the town after we have a meeting with Nena on the latest styles and trends. So Nena, bring us up to speed. A few hours later. While, I certainly did not realize the life beings were so focused on the exterior coverings. At least we can just morph outfits as needed. Using only one true covering. That true. Now it's time for the partying to begin. Where shall we go? A few of my co-workers suggested Club Carnival in New Shibuya. New Shibuya here we come. Loud music in the back ground and a roaring crowd cheering on the hottest band around, Chop Stix. Shaila, who are your friends? These are not just my friends, but these are my siblings. Really. You all look to be about the same age. We get that a lot. I am the eldest. Then there is Randy, pointing him out. Over here is my brother Brock, who will be leaving soon for the police academy. Next there is Breana, she's the doctor of the family. Ciara here is next and last but not least the twins Justin and Justice our University students. Welcome to New Shibuya. And welcome to club carnival. Have you guys heard Chop Stix play live before. No never. We are from New Memphis. New Memphis. I have never been that far north. I hear it's a long journey. Yes it is. What brings you all here? We just needed a new start. Our parents passed and we couldn't stand being anywhere in Perdida. I'm sorry to hear about your loss. Oh, it's okay now. It happened during the war. I see. Here's to new beginnings then. To new beginnings. Shaila may I have this dance? I'm not much of a dancer, but I'll try. Via telepathy, Nena help. Downloading the latest dance moves sweeping New Shibuya. The peacock swing and you said you couldn't dance. You are full of surprises Shaila. Thanks Vincent. I am so glad you invited me out tonight. So am I. That was simply amazing. You can really move Vincent. Thank you, but I must say, I didn't want to be left in the dust. So are they doing the peacock swing in New Memphis? Actually we call it the through back. I'll get us something to drink. What would you like? Why don't you surprise me? Okay, I'll pick something stellar and smooth, just like you. Justin check out Bill and Mattie. Where? To your left. Your other Left. You mean my right? Oh, yeah. I think we need to go and say hello? Yes, I agree. Justin, what are you doing here? Justice and I are here with our family celebrating. What's the occasion? Our brother Brock is leaving for the police academy. That's really good news. It is very hard to make the cut nowadays. Bill you remember Justin and his sister Justice from school. Yes. Justice and Justin. You are twins aren't you? Yes, fraternal twins. Of course you are. Why don't you and Mattie come join us over here with our family and some new friends from work? That's very kind of you. Were you all meeting anyone else? No, no one in particular. Were just hanging out. You see, Mattie and I are neighbors. We have known each other all our lives and we have this brother sister thing going on. Yeah, it's a brother sister thing. Are you all dating anyone? Who me and Justice? No we are both single as well. Everyone this is Mattie and Bill. Mattie and Bill meet everyone. Which of you is going to the academy? That'll be me. My name is Brock. Congratulations Brock. Thanks Bill, I appreciate that. We need solid citizens to keep the people of New Persepolis safe and with a peace of mind. There are very few people to take on such a noble mission. That is true. My father is a vet. So is Mattie's. Is that right? What did your dad do for the military? Both our dads served in a top secret capacity. To be honest, neither of us knows exactly what they did, but it must have been very significant. Boy, I would have liked to be a fly on the wall back in those days. There is no telling what secrets we would uncover. I would like to meet your fathers someday, perhaps when I am done with my training. Mattie and I will see what we can do. That'll be great. Where are the military bases? There are no more bases. We now have sentries to do the protecting. They are very reliable. This keeps us from having to actually get into physical battles. After world war three, there were so many lives lost. So the league of Chancellors decided it would be best to allow the sentry program to assume the military to cut back on the death toll. Now it is easier to settle disputes. To be quite honest disputes are long over. They are virtually none existent today. Also we're all on one giant plain which makes it nearly impossible to have war which will end all life as we know it. So then the peace treaties begin and here we are. There is a lot more to it, but that's just a brief synopsis. I suppose I'm boring you with the history lesson? No, not at all. Are you a history major as well? No, I just read a lot of history. Maybe someday, you and I could sit down and talk about it a little more in depth? Sure, I will keep myself available for you to call. How about next weekend on Saturday? That suits me fine. Doctor Collier, it's me Daniel Landers. Doctor Landers from the Institute. Oh, I didn't recognize you without the smock. I couldn't miss you. Thanks. I didn't think you were the type to spend time in New Shibuya, that alone club carnival. Actually I'm here with my family and some friends. Care to join us? Yes, if it is no inconvenience to you all? Don't be silly, it will be our pleasure. Everyone, this is an associate of mine from work Dan. Dan these are our friends Vincent, Debra, Bill and Mattie. These are my bothers Brock, Randy and Justin. And my sisters Shaila, Ciara and Justice. Hello everyone, nice to meet you all. Same here. Likewise. What are you drinking Dan? Nothing actually. I don't indulge. Neither do I. I was starting to feel like the lone wolf here. Certainly I am glad to no longer be alone. Well dear girl consider us joined at the hip. I do dance though. Would you like to dance? Sure, I think I can shake a tail feather. Feet don't fail me now. Nena, some help please. I need something other than the peacock. Shaila has surely become the queen of it. Something a little less flamboyant. Yes Breana, I have something just your speed the rattle tat. Superb. Go ahead and add a style for each of us severally as well Nena. Consider it done. Guys the probes are approaching. There are literally thousands of them heading for New Shibuya. What's going on Nena. I don't know, but I think all of you need to get your friends to cover and then ready for battle. Are you sure that is necessary. I'm positive. The probes are in war mode. I'm just not sure what their target is. Since you are now known to some life beings, I suggest you implore Tristan and Anu. That will help to keep your true identity concealed. Thanks for the dance Dan. We all have to leave now. So soon, the night is still tender. Yes, but we promised Brock, we would all leave earlier to help him maintain his level of readiness. I apologize to all of you for being such a stick in the mud. Please forgive me. Of course Brock, we know you're leaving next week, so better get home to bed then said Dan, with a coy grin. I suppose we all have to get going. Right, Bill those classes are pretty darn demanding. I tell you what Dan, you are good for a reign check. Now that's something I'll look forward to. So long ladies and gents, until we meet again. Now implore Anu. Shaila, Breana, Ciara and Justice morph. With a flash of dazzling light the four become one. I am Anu defender of the Milky Way. Now implore Tristan. Brock, Randy and Justin morph. I am Tristan defender of the Milky Way. The twin defenders leap into action above the clouds hidden from the probes to see what the threat maybe. Then there was a sonic bum from below and two thirds of the probe fell from the sky plummeting to the earth. A sea of fire and smoke over take the sky so Tristan and Anu come down for a closer look. In the distance they see a powerful being destroying the remainder of the probes. Tristan attack. Anu comes in first with a blow to the beast's head. Tristan follows with a one two punch to the torso. The beast is able to get back to his feet and open up an assault on Tristan with a laser beam from the eyes and fire from the mouth. Anu counter attacks with her laser and severs the head of the beast from its shoulders. When the head touches the ground it breaks off into millions of lesser creatures and fan out beneath the earth's surface. The same became of the torso with no trace of the beast to be found. The crowd is in awe at the sight of the two giants' battle realizing the heroes are Tristan and Anu. To keep the mystery going Tristan and Anu race away to the clouds and disappear from the sight of the people below. Back aboard Nena Tristan and Anu review the memory reels to see if they can learn anything new regarding the attack. They study and study with no avail. The twins realize that the collective may be able to see something that the two of them missed. I believe this is a good time for us to call upon the collective to review the reels to insure every angle has been covered. Yes, Anu I gree. I call Justin, Brock and Randy from the collective. With dazzling light the three brothers emerge. I call Breana,Shaila,Justice and Ciara from the collective. And the girls appear after the same effects. Now, let's take a closer look. Nena, do you have any new developments on the captured probe? Yes, I have been able to determine that the probe is manmade. The life beings attacked us? But why? Shaila, I believe it was not an assult on friendlies. What I mean is, the probes are design to protect the interest of the life beings. To them, we are a threat. Remember, we aren't of this galaxy. We are alien. Foreign to everything they know. There is a threat to their life. A real threat. So this is the cause of their attack on Ciara. No other reason. I agree. So do we all? Yes, I believe we all agree Shaila. Then we must move on from this point. What about this creature. The creature is also manmade, but a synthetic being. How is that possible? The humans are less advance than we were on Shumaria, but none the less very astute beings. Someone has constructed this weapon to bring harm from within the earth. Why would the humans create something that would   speed up the possibility of their own destruction? I don't think that's what has happened. Remember all life beings aren't aware offury's fire. Only the elite have this information. The enemy may or may not be aware of the issue. Regardless of the fact that this so called enemy knows or doesn't know is beside the point. We simple have to uncover his plot and foil his plan. Where do we even begin? This is a very daunting process. Maybe, we can begin with the other military installations. As an investigative reporter, I can go in and dig up as much information as I can under the guise of a conspiracy theory regarding the attack on sector one. Shaila, have you forgotten that we destroyed sector one? Yeah Shaila, we did that to rescue Ciara. Yes, yes I know. The thing is do they know. Isn't that kind of a risky thoug You may have to act alone. Not entirely true. We have other allies now. We have our friends. Shaila, I don't know about this. We are supposed to keep the life beings out of harm's way, not bring them face to face with death and doom. Listen, the more I get to know the life beings, the more I realize that we have to rely on them for this mission to be successful. I know that they would want to fight for their future if they knew the threat. That is the very purpose of having an army. Yes, but that is an army of probes, none life beings. Ciara, you were the one that said we can't do this alone. We must consider the best possible outcome of this battle first. We know why we are doing this. It is for their sakes. Besides, the life beings are more resourceful than we give them credit for. At any rate, I want be alone and will have some allies. Nena will be on stand by and so will all of you. I can reach you via telepathy in seconds if I'm in any real danger. This is an order and it stands. leaving the room to end the conversation, Shaila takes a deep breath and carries on. I hope she knows what she is doing? So do we all. Mr. Sinclaire. Uh, Shaila, how are you doing? Fine, thank you. Please have a seat? Thanks. I really had a great time last night Shaila. So did I Mr. Sinclaire. Shaila, Mr. Sinclaire is my father, please call me Vincent. Sure Vincent. Well, Vincent. I'm here because my sources tell me that there was an explosion at one of the military station housing the probes and thousands of probes were destroyed. Okay, go on. Well, I was wondering if there may be a connection between that incident and the one last night at New Shibuya. You know Shaila, actually that's a very good question. Yes, that's why I'm a reporter. To be quite honest with you, I had the same thoughts. I am willing to compare notes, if you are. Notes, so you are already working on this case. Well, I didn't see any reason not to gather info so that when I came to you with an offer I would seem more creditable. That's very astute of you. Shaila, don't be frightened by my comments. I just haven't anything to compare. You are miles ahead of me already. I'm still in the thinking process right now. What will you say if I give you lead on this story and I back you up? I was hoping you would say that or something to that affect. Do you now. Yes. I was looking forward to seeing you again. Now we will get to spend some time together. Well Ms. Collier, that is music to me ears. I'm very flattered that you have an interest in spending time with me. Perhaps we can have a little lunch while we talk things over. Say in about an hour or an hour and a half. Yep, that sounds just fine. In that case meet back here outside my office at ten fort five. Okay, I'll be here. This must be my lucky day said Vinnie. He is so adorable thought Shaila. I wonder what he would do if he ever found out I'm synthetic. I'm sure it would change things altogether. Okay young lady focus on the mission and not the man. Teleporting from a restroom stall back to Nena in orbit. So, I take it that went well. Did you hear all of that Nena? Yes, Shaila. I hear every word that you say or think when I'm near the sun. Oh, I guess I have to get use to that. I was not eaves dropping Shaila. It just is. I know Nena. It's just we were having a private moment. Since you know, what is your opinion? My opinion on what exactly? You know? Vincent and I. I think I'm developing the love. Shaila, that is highly likely since you are becoming more human like with each day. The thing is, I will never truly be able to be his. I mean, I'm not what he thinks I am. I feel like a fraud. I don't like this feeling. Good, it is not a feeling one should enjoy. It is however a feeling one must learn from. This is only the beginning of you transformation. You are like a beautiful flower at spring time. Be patient and anxious for nothing. In due time things will work themselves out. You will see. Hello Shaila, Hello Nena. You are home early Justice. Yes, I finished my classes for today. Where is Justin? He is still in class. He has a more rigorous schedule than I. He will be another couple of hours yet. What did I interrupt here? Oh, nothing. It didn't seem that way to me. What did you here Justice? I heard nothing, but I really since there is something a foot here. Oh, in that case we were just talking about the mission. Right, whatever. I suppose you have more information about what you're doing? No, not exactly. I have a date with Vincent and we will be coming up with some sort of strategy as to how we will proceed. That's excellent. I will get some lunch and head out to the mall. I plan to meet Mattie and some of the other girls and see what I can shake from the bush. That is good Justice. Yes, I took my queue from yours truly. You should be proud? I am very proud my dear. Aren't you proud as well Nena? Yes mam, certainly. Thank you ladies for that lovely dialogue, but I must hurry along. What about your lunch? I grab some at the mall. looks like you two need some privacy. You know what they say, three is a crowd. What was that all about Nena? It's call jealousy captain. Jealousy. Of what. You and I being friends. We are friends yes. Yes, but she is my sister. Yes, but she doesn't understand the dynamics of our relationship opposed to hers. I think she and I get along great. Yes you do. Then why is this a problem for her? This is something she will have to face on her own. You are the eldest, but you can't protect them from all of the hurts and disappointments they will face. You have to be strong enough to allow them to make their own mistakes. Ym.rtoll is to lead and guide. I just don't want anyone to get hurt. Exactly, that's what I just said. let go. You are all the same, even though your coping mechanisms are set as the eldest, you still have to have failed experiences yourself to fully understand others in the same or similar situations. And you Nena? What about you. I have the wisdom of Dr. Collier. He wanted me to act in this capacity for your sake and the others. I am not capable of jealousy. My heart is fixed to do what I was created to do without natural affection. You see, I will never. I cannot be human ever. I am an adjutant and that alone is my purpose here. I accept it whole heartedly.

CHAPTER 4

UNCHARTERED

Mattie, I'm over here. Hello Justice. I want you to meet Pearl and Diamond they are twins, and this is Sandy Cook. My sister Madeline and her friend Sara. So where are we going. Well, I thought we would grab some coffee and scones at Butler's. Then chat about a road trip to the coast. Doesn't a beach trip sound refresh right now. We can sail and scuba drive and such. You work harder, you play even harder.

All work and no play make Mattie a dull girl. There will be boys there too. Maybe we can introduce you to someone there or I'm sure you will have no trouble meeting someone. This is all kind of new to me. Oh, are you shy? Didn't you have a boyfriend back in the north. I see that's it. You already have a dream boat. Hum! Is he tall, dark and handsome? Joking and laughing as they walk the city block to their destination. Justice not sure what to say or think, has no response just a coy smile of embarrassment. Mattie grabs her hand in assurance that she means no harm. I'm only kidding. Don't be too serious.

Lighten up a little will you. Come on, let's have some fun. Justice realizing the serious look on her face then smiles.

Acknowledging Mattie with a head signal yes. Then says okay I'm in. Good, said Mattie. You won't regret it. Meanwhile, back on-board Nena in orbit just outside of earth's gravitational pull. The boys are working on a project of their own. Brock, the idea is preposterous. We can have the nanoids configure an approximation of the trajectory for us while.we are in sleep stasis. I guess you are right Randy, but we must test it out as soon as possible before we present the idea to Shaila. I don't think she will have a problem with the suggestion. Just make sure all the perimeters for the plan are ironed out. Let's walk through it step by step one more time. Briana, what are those three up too. I don't know but they are being very secretive about it. I haven't been able to ascertain exactly what it is. All I know is they have oeen at it all day. Have you two girls seen Justice today asked Shaila. No replied Ciara. I think she went to meet Mattie and some of her friends said Briana. I wonder what they are up to. I don't know, but she is trying to blend in with the college crowd. I'll have Justice drop in on her in a little bit to see if she is ok. I think she may be trying to develop a sense of independence from the collective. Is that so wrong Shaila asked Ciara. No. No not at all. I believe we all need our separate identities. In fact, I'm going to call Vincent to set up a date for tomorrow. I really need to speak with him about my findings.

Back on earth, Mattie and the girls have planned their beach outing and are headed back to their varying locations. "I really enjoyed the time and discussion said Mattie. With a great smile on her face. Justice acknowledges with her head. Then says So did I. I am looking forward to the trip. You know Justice, you really should invite your brother Justin to come as well. Oh, okay. I'm sure he will like that. Yeah. My brother and some of the guys from school will be there. Perhaps he would like to join them in some of the outdoor activities. That sounds delightful. I'll be sure to bring it to his attention as soon as I see him. Just in that moment from orbit arrives Justin in a stall inside a clothing boutique near where the girls are disbursing from. Hello handsome, we were just talking about you. "What are you doing here asked Justice. This is my girl's day out. Just us girls remember! Yeah, sure Justice, I was just out shopping. Maybe I can take you to the house. Shaila has been wondering where you are. Isn't that your sister though? Not your mom? Right. Yes, she is only my sister. Our eldest sister though, explained Justin. She looks out for all of us, and our parents left her in charge. Oh. I see. Well, I hope we haven't gotten you in any trouble. No, not at all. She is just looking out for me is all. I'll talk to you later. Yes, give me a call when you get home. We need to talk about clothes for the trip. Okay. Why are you stalking me? Shaila began to worry and sent me to make sure you are ok. I'm ok. I just need my own space. We can't do everything together. I am tired of being without privacy. Nena can hear all our conversations! We can connect. There is no sense of privacy for us. Have you considered bringing this up to everyone? What would be the point! No one cares but me. I care too. I am aware of the same things. Look. I understand that you are frustrated with why we are designed. But there are so many advantages to it as well. Besides, Nena is very protective of our personal space. I suppose you are right. I'm just irritated! Come on my darling better half. Everything will be alright. I feel better having expressed my frustration with someone out loud. So how are things? Did you and the girls formulate a plan for your weekend getaway. We certainly did and what's more Mattie asked you to join us as well. Why? Why not? This is a chance for me to be with the in-crowd. Don't blow this for me. Really? Blow it for you. I'm the cool one over here. The alpha male on campus. What do you mean blow it for you. Don't blow it! said Justin. No, you! said Justice. Both smiling and enjoying twindom.

I was going to wait for Justin to return before I presented this idea Shaila, but I see no need to wait. Randy, Justin and I think that we can have the nanoids configure a trajectory approximation while we are asleep. The nanoids asked Shaila? Yes nanoids. They will have full capability of power as long as Nena orbits in the shadow of the sun. So, you all have given this idea a lot of thought. I will take it under advisement, and I'll give you a decision soon. Have you run any scenarios to see if your hypothesis will work? No not yet. We wanted to address the idea with you before testing to have your approval.

I see. Go ahead with the trials. Get back with the results and we will go from there. So that's a go then. For now. Yes, it's a go. Trials only though. Yes madam. Trials only. Great job Brock and Randy. Great job. She likes it. Yes, Randy, she gave us the go ahead. Both guys have a look of accomplishment as they talk & continue working and exploring their ideas. So that was interesting. They just wanted to present an idea. Honestly, it's a great idea. So of course, I said yes, but I'm making them work for it though. You should see the expressions on their faces when I said, yes. The boys are so easy and so wonderful. I can hardly contain myself. Captain. Yes Nena, the boys are coming into their own. You will find that the girls will have to find other methods of separate fulfilment. Justice has an outlet with her school friends. It will be a good idea to have the other girls pour themselves into their work as well. Nena, do you know something I don't? No. it's just an observation. Each one of you needs to find your own way. This is a part of the growth process. You are growing and changing and will need your own individuality as time progresses. Do you trust me Shaila. Shaila Nena, very much so. My only function is to aid you and the crew. I've been thinking about that though Nena. If we are becoming more humanoid, why is that not the same function for you. My anatomic make up and yours is different in that I am completely synthetic, whereas you all have part DNA from Doctor Collier. He did not construct me the same way. And although I am evolving, it is a different process for me. Don't worry, I am content with the process. For

I know well my position. My esoteric form was Doctor Collier's brilliance at work. And I can look outwardly human but will never achieve an actual human make up physically. I am the adjutant. Besides, I will always need to be a part of the ship for deep space explorations and research. My programing is the unique analysis of Doctor Collier and his assistant Margret combined. Their training and experiences were copied from their DNA to my nanite circuitry embedded with a DNA particle from each host that stimulates my personality. So, in essence you have human parts. Only the spec of blood from each host. You have something then. You have something! I appreciate the enthusiasm, though I doubt it will make for anything more than just mere discussion. Have you worn the exoskeletal body yet? No, there hasn't been a need for me to dawn the droid. Perhaps you need to spend some time in your own skin, this will help you to develop along with the rest of us. Perhaps said Nena. Then, it's settled. Take it out for a spin. Captain. I have so much to focus on. Yes, you do, but I happen to know you are complex and can operate all your systems from either compartment simultaneously. You are stalling Nena Collier. Dawn the droid. Young Lady, that's an order. Captain? Yes Captain. Now for the first time Nena explores from within her droid. She takes a quick tour near the sun and then cloaks herself to explore the underdeveloped parts of rural earth. Taken in the view of the singular large mass surrounded by the great body of water. The seven hundred years have not only changed the landscape of earth, but the ecological make up is also different in many ways. Giant terrifying creatures roam the underdeveloped parts of land and in the sea. Some speculate that they are of alien origin and not indigenous to the earth. Nena begins an analysis of the origin of the creatures to present the study to Shaila and the team for further review.

A few days later at the beach resort in Port Venice of New Persepolis, Justice and Justin meet with the other students for their sabbatical. Have you ever seen such perfection Justice, asked Mattie. It is so calming here near the waters. The sentry has been set up to keep this region of waters pure and unsullied by the creatures that roam underneath. It is even rumored that they have come upon land in page certain outskirts of rural areas added Diamond. Savage beast. Some say they are creatures awakened from the deep. They lay dormant beneath the earth's crust until the great quakes of 2543. Who knows the actual truth, I mean technology has just in the recent past 200 or so years been restored and at the level we know it today. We are far more advanced than our ancestral counterparts. Study shows we live at least twenty years longer today than in their day. My sister Pearl has worked out a study of ancient earth. Particularly Asia and Europe. Can you imagine everything being spread out. Having to fly here and there. Or the distance they had to travel to get to some areas? But now we can be in any state in less than four hours from point to point. You can drive clear across the entire continent in three days. Nonstop of course. I think that is fascinating. You have your mountain ranges and your valleys. Your rain forests and the desert. Then there's the ocean fronts. In just sixty more years people will be living on the moon and mars. As for me though, just give me planet earth. She is home forever. Sandy? Asked Mattie, you wouldn't take a trip to the moon if you could. I would absolutely kill for an opportunity like that. Sandy responds. No No. I'm a creature of comfort. I've needs that can only be met here on earth. Suit yourself. If I had a chance, I would be so gone, said Diamond. Bring the bring and all its solitary grace and splendor. To each his own ladies said Bill. Hello everyone. It's nice to see you again Justin. Hello yourself, Bill. I hear you have moved to a new apartment in town. Yes. Yes. I thought it was high time for me to get out on my own. Have you seen my new wheels? I'll take you for a spin sometime. Just let know when, and we can head out. Sounds like fun. I just love this song. The artist is so beautiful. Her music just moves me. My favorite song from the album. Loves sweet melody in my heart. It's a special work of art. Poetry for the soul. "Do you follow this artist Justin asked Mattie. No, I'm sorry I'm not familiar with her work. You guys must get out more. Just listen to the sweet sounds and the melody. It's simply beautiful. Don't you think. Since you put it like that, why yes ma'am. There are so many beautiful things I see. I mean in the song of course. Of course, agreed Mattie. The girls were snickering. Oh, brother come on Justin before you get bitten by the bug. The bug asked Justin. Yes, love bug. It's contagious. The group all laugh and begin to enjoy the festivities.

Mattie, I'm over here. Hello Justice. I want you to meet Pearl and Diamon d they are twins, and this is Sandy Cook. My sister Madeline and her friend Sara. So where are we going. Well, I thought we would grab some coffee and scones at Butler's. Then chat about a road trip to the coast. Doesn't a beach trip sound refresh right now. We can sail and scuba drive and such. You work harder, you play even harder.

All work and no play make Mattie a dull girl. There will be boys there too. Maybe we can introduce you to someone there or I'm sure you will have no trouble meeting someone. This is all kind of new to me. Oh, are you shy? Didn't you have a boyfriend back in the north. I see that's it. You already have a dream boat. Hum! Is he tall, dark and handsome? Joking and laughing as they walk the city block to their destination. Justice not sure what to say or think, has no response just a coy smile of embarrassment. Mattie grabs her hand in assurance that she means no harm. I'm only kidding. Don't be too serious. Lighten up a little will you. Come on, let's have some fun. Justice realizing the serious look on her face then smiles. Acknowledging Mattie with a head signal yes. Then says okay I'm in. Good, said Mattie. You won't regret it. Meanwhile, back on-board Nena in orbit just outside of earth's gravitational pull. The boys are working on a project of their own. Brock, the idea is preposterous. We can have the nanoids configure an approximation of the trajectory for us while we are in sleep stasis. I guess you are right Randy, but we must test it out as soon as possible before we present the idea to Shaila. I don't think she will have a problem with the suggestion. Just make sure all the perimeters for the plan are ironed out. Let's walk through it step by step one more time. Briana, what are those three up too. I don't know but they are being very secretive about it. I haven't been able to ascertain exactly what it is. All I know is they have been at it all day. Have you two girls seen Justice today asked Shaila. No replied Ciara. I think she went to meet Mattie and some of her friends said Briana. I wonder what they are up to. I don't know, but she is trying to blend in with the college crowd. I'll have Justice drop in on her in a litle bit to see if she is ok. I think she may be trying to develop a sense of independence from the collective. Is that so wrong Shaila asked Ciara. No. No not at all. I believe we all need our separate identities. In fact, I'm going to call Vincent to set up a date for tomorrow. I really need to speak with him about my findings.

Back on earth, Mattie and the girls have planned their beach outing and are headed back to their varying locations. "I really enjoyed the time and discussion said Mattie. With a great smile on her face. Justice acknowledges with her head. Then says So did I. I am looking forward to the trip. You know Justice, you really should invite your brother Justin to come as well. Oh, okay. I'm sure he will like that. Yeah. My brother and some of the guys from school will be there. Perhaps he would like to join them in some of the outdoor activities. That sounds delightful.

I'll be sure to bring it to his attention as soon as I see him. Just in that moment from orbit arrives Justin in a stall inside a clothing boutique near where the girls are disbursing from. Hello handsome, we were just talking about you. "What are you doing here asked Justice. This is my girl's day out. Just us girls remember! Yeah, sure Justice, I was just out shopping. Maybe I can take you to the house. Shaila has been wondering where you are. Isn't that your sister though? Not your mom? Right. Yes, she is only my sister. Our eldest sister though, explained Justin. She looks out for all of us, and our parents left her in charge. Oh. I see. Well, I hope we haven't gotten you in any trouble. No, not at all. She is just looking out for me is all. I'll talk to you later. Yes, give me a call when you get home. We need to talk about clothes for the trip. Okay. Why are you stalking me? Shaila began to worry and sent me to make sure you are ok. I'm ok. I just need my own space. We can't do everything together. I am tired of being without privacy. Nena can hear all our conversations! We can connect. There is no sense of privacy for us. Have you considered bringing this up to everyone? What would be the point! No one cares but me. I care too. I am aware of the same things. Look. I understand that you are frustrated with why we are designed. But there are so many advantages to it as well. Besides, Nena is very protective of our personal space. I suppose you are right. I'm just irritated! Come on my darling better half. Everything will be alright. I feel better having expressed my frustration with someone out loud. So how are things? Did you and the girls formulate a plan for your weekend getaway. We certainly did and what's more Mattie asked you to join us as well. Why? Why not? This is a chance for me to be with the in-crowd. Don't blow this for me. Really? Blow it for you. I'm the cool one over here. The alpha male on campus. What do you mean blow it for you. Don't blow it! said Justin. No, you! said Justice. Both smiling and enjoying twindom.

I was going to wait for Justin to return before I presented this idea Shaila, but I see no need to wait. Randy, Justin and I think that we can have the nanoids configure a trajectory approximation while we are asleep. The nanoids asked Shaila? Yes nanoids. They will have full capability of power as long as Nena orbits in the shadow of the sun. So, you all have given this idea a lot of thought. I will take it under advisement, and I'll give you a decision soon. Have you run any scenarios to see if your hypothesis will work? No not yet. We wanted to address the idea with you before testing to have your approval. I see. Go ahead with the trials. Get back with the results and we will go from there. So that's a go then. For now. Yes, it's a go. Trials only though. Yes madam. Trials only. Great job Brock and Randy. Great job. She likes it. Yes, Randy, she gave us the go ahead. Both guys have a look of accomplishment as they talk & continue working and exploring their ideas. So that was interesting. They just wanted to present an idea. Honestly, it's a great idea. So of course, I said yes, but I'm making them work for it though. You should see the expressions on their faces when I said, yes. The boys are so easy and so wonderful.

I can hardly contain myself. Captain. Yes Nena, the boys are coming into their own. You will find that the girls will have to find other methods of separate fulfilment. Justice has an outlet with her school friends. It will be a good Idea to have the other girls pour themselves into their work as well. Nena, do you know something I don't? No. it's just an observation. Each one of you needs to find your own way. This is a part of the growth process. You are growing and changing and will need your own individuality as time progresses. Do you trust me Shaila. Shaila Nena, very much so. My only function is to aid you and the crew. I've been thinking about that though Nena. If we are becoming more humanoid, why is that not the same function for you. My anatomic make up and yours is different in that I am completely synthetic, whereas you all have part DNA from Doctor Collier. He did not construct me the same way. And although I am evolving, it is a different process for me. Don't worry, I am content with the process. For I know well my position. My esoteric form was Doctor Collier's brilliance at work. And I can look outwardly human but will never achieve an actual human make up physically. I am the adjutant. Besides, I will always need to be a part of the ship for deep space explorations and research. My programing is the unique analysis of Doctor Collier and his assistant Margret combined. Their training and experiences were copied from their DNA to my nanite circuitry embedded with a DNA particle from each host that stimulates my personality. So, in essence you have human parts. Only the spec of blood from each host.

You have something then. You have something! I appreciate the enthusiasm, though I doubt it will make for anything more than just mere discussion. Have you worn the exoskeletal body yet? No, there hasn't been a need for me to dawn the droid. Perhaps you need to spend some time in your own skin, this will help you to develop along with the rest of us. Perhaps said Nena. Then, it's settled. Take it out for a spin. Captain. I have so much to focus on. Yes, you do, but I happen to know you are complex and can operate all your systems from either compartment simultaneously. You are stalling Nena Collier. Dawn the droid. Young Lady, that's an order. Captain? Yes Captain. Now for the first time Nena explores from within her droid. She takes a quick tour near the sun and then cloaks herself to explore the underdeveloped parts of rural earth. Taken in the view of the singular large mass surrounded by the great body of water. The seven hundred years have not only changed the landscape of earth, but the ecological make up is also different in many ways. Giant terrifying creatures roam the underdeveloped parts of land and in the sea. Some speculate that they are of alien origin and not indigenous to the earth. Nena begins an analysis of the origin of the creatures to present the study to Shaila and the team for further review.

A few days later at the beach resort in Port Venice of New Persepolis, Justice and Justin meet with the other students for their sabbattical. Have you ever seen such perfection Justice, asked Mattie. It is so calming here near the waters. The sentry has been set up to keep this region of waters pure and unsullied by the creatures that roam underneath. It is even rumored that they have come upon land in page certain outskirts of rural areas added Diamond. Savage beast. Some say they are creatures awakened from the deep. They lay dormant beneath the earth's crust until the great quakes of 2543. Who knows the actual truth, I mean technology has just in the recent past 200 or so years been restored and at the level we know it today. We are far more advanced than our ancestral counterparts. Study shows we live at least twenty years longer today than in their day. My sister Pearl has worked out a study of ancient earth. Particularly Asia and Europe. Can you imagine everything being spread out. Having to fly here and there. Or the distance they had to travel to get to some areas? But now we can be in any state in less than four hours from point to point. You can drive clear across the entire continent in three days. Nonstop of course. I think that is fascinating. You have your mountain ranges and your valleys. Your rain forests and the desert. Then there's the ocean fronts. In just sixty more years people will be living on the moon and mars. As for me though, just give me planet earth. She is home forever. Sandy? Asked Mattie, you wouldn't take a trip to the moon if you could. I would absolutely kill for an opportunity like that. Sandy responds. No No. I'm a creature of comfort. I've needs that can only be met here on earth. Suit yourself. If I had a chance, I would be so gone, said Diamond. Bring the bring and all its solitary grace and splendor. To each his own ladies said Bill. Hello everyone. It's nice to see you again Justin. Hello yourself, Bill. I hear you have moved to a new apartment in town. Yes. Yes. I thought it was high time for me to get out on my own. Have you seen my new wheels? I'll take you for a spin sometime. Just let know when, and we can head out. Sounds like fun. I just love this song. The artist is so beautiful. Her music just moves me. My favorite song from the album. Loves sweet melody in my heart. It's a special work of art. Poetry for the soul. "Do you follow this artist Justin asked Mattie. No, I'm sorry I'm not familiar with her work. You guys must get out more. Just listen to the sweet sounds and the melody. It's simply beautiful. Don't you think. Since you put it like that, why yes ma'am. There are so many beautiful things I see. I mean in the song of course. Of course, agreed Mattie. The girls were snickering. Oh, brother come on Justin before you get biten by the bug. The bug asked Justin. Yes, love bug. It's contagious. The group all laugh and begin to enjoy the festivities.